E
KEL

Kellogg, Steven.

Aster Aardvark's
alphabet
adventures.

$13.88

69BT00885

E
KEL

Kellogg, Steven.

Aster Aardvark's
alphabet
adventures.

$13.88

69BT00885

DATE	BORROWER'S NAME	

© THE BAKER & TAYLOR CO.

ASTER
AARDVARK'S
ALPHABET
ADVENTURES

· STEVEN KELLOGG ·

ASTER
AARDVARK'S
ALPHABET
ADVENTURES

· MORROW JUNIOR BOOKS ·

NEW YORK

For everyone I love,
from **A**my Larson to **Z**ack Porter

Printed in the United States of America.
2 3 4 5 6 7 8 9
Library of Congress Cataloging-in-Publication Data
Kellogg, Steven.
Aster Aardvark's alphabet adventures.
Summary: Alliterative text and pictures present
adventures of animals from A to Z.
[1. Animals—Fiction. 2. Alphabet. 3. Alliteration.]
I. Title.
PZ7.K292As   1987   [E]   87-5715
ISBN 0-688-07256-9
ISBN 0-688-07257-7 (lib. bdg.)

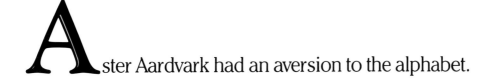

Aster Aardvark had an aversion to the alphabet.

Appalled by Aster's attitude, Acorn Acres Academy alerted her aunt Agnes, who arranged for an airplane to aid Aster's academic advancement.

After Aster applied herself and achieved an A, all assembled to applaud her amazing aptitude for aerial alphabetical acrobatics.

Bertha Bear and her Brooklyn buddies were being bothered by a bratty baboon who baited them as a bunch of basketball bums. "Beat it, blockhead! Someday we'll be big on Broadway," Bertha bawled.

Before long, Bertha, Bettina, Barbette, and Belinda were booked by the Bijou, where they bounded across the boards in a basketball ballet. From the balcony the boars bombarded them with blossoms while the bison below bellowed, "Bravo!"

Cheering continued at the concert as Canadian conductor Cyril Capon cleverly coordinated a chorus of caterwauling cats, croaking condors, cawing crows, cackling cardinals, cooing cuckoos, chattering chickens, crooning crocodiles, and coloratura cows.

Desperate for dinner after a day of digging up dinosaurs in the desert, Dr. Delphius Dog and a dozen dedicated disciples dined on delicious delicacies delivered by a duo of distinguished ducks dangling from a dirigible.

Entering an elite eating establishment escorted by an enormously eminent elephant, Estelle Egret encountered eight ermines who ecstatically extolled the elegance of her eyeglasses and the excellence of each emerald in her earrings, and then earnestly entreated her to elope.

lashbulbs flickered and frenzied fans fainted as famous Fred Freeble, fullback for the Fresno Furies, was festooned with feathers for the flight footage in Flora Flamingo's first feature film, *The Flying Fox of Football*. Unfortunately, the finale was a flop because Fred failed to fly and fell flapping into the fountain.

Gregory Grizzly and a group of gorillas had gathered for golf when a gaggle of geese in goggles and gaudy gowns galloped onto the green. Gregory grumbled as the geese gaily gamboled, but the gorillas gradually grinned, then giggled and guffawed in glorious giddiness.

H

ermione, a hefty hyperactive hippo, hurt her hip hurling herself into the Hawaiian Hula Hoop Happening.

She hobbled home to heal in her handmade hammock. However, her hip hindered her from hopping in, so the hapless hippo hollered hysterically.

Happily, hibernating Harris Hare heard her howling and hastened to help, heroically heaving Hermione head over heels into the hammock.

I nfatuated with Iris Ibis, the illustrious ice skater, Irving Iguana inquired at her island igloo, but an intern icily insisted that Iris was indefinitely indisposed and an interview was impossible.

The iguana ignored this information and impulsively introduced itself to Iris, who was inspired by its invitation to indulge immoderately in ice cream.

J

ust before joining the Japanese jaguars in a jostling judo joust, the jolly jackrabbits juggled jellybeans.

Then they jogged through the jungle and jumped into the Jacuzzi, where they jabbered and joked and enjoyed jars of jam.

Kenilworth, the kind kangaroo, kissed his kin Katherine Koala, who had kept his kite and his kitchen key in her kayak.

L ana, a lazy lioness from Louisiana, launched into a long, loud lecture lashing the little lemurs for lining the lagoon with laundry.

Finally, as lanterns were lit, her lackeys lifted her litter and lurched across the lawn to lunch at Lily Leopard's.

But Lana was so late not a lick of lunch was left.

Marchmain Mouse misplaced his monocle on a museum mission in Mexico. He meandered miserably in the mountains for months until a mummified mailman on a motorbike materialized, moaning, "Mark my message from Martha." The mouse was mortified. "Martha? Martha who?" he muttered.

Marchmain marveled as the messenger magically metamorphosed into Martha Mole, whom he'd met at the marble matches in Malta last May. Moreover, Martha maintained she meant to marry him on Monday!

N

ero, a natty newt from North Newport, was a notorious nuisance in his neighborhood until he was nabbed nailing a net over the nest where Ned Nightingale napped.

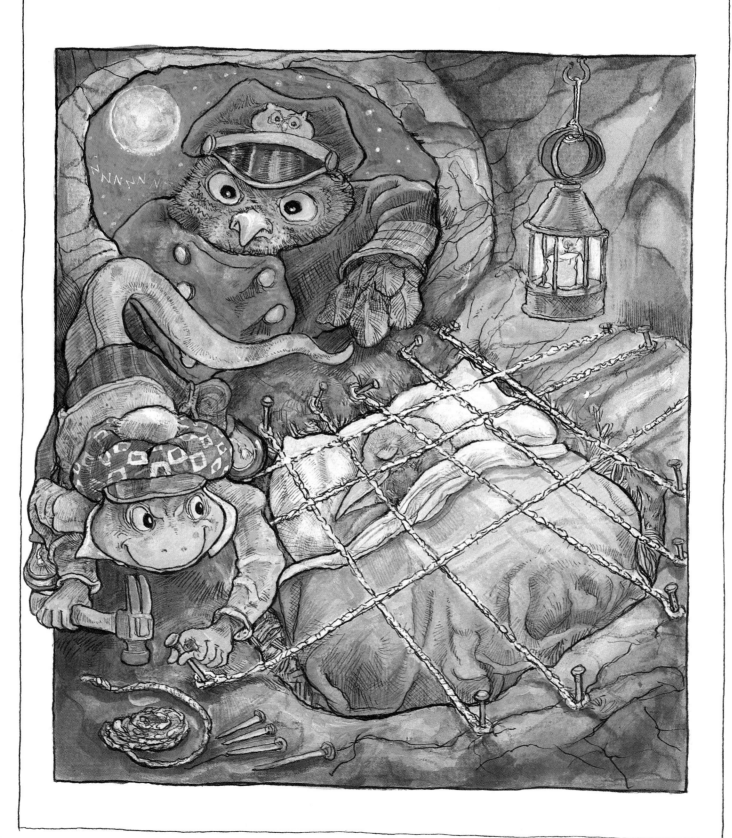

O utraged by the otter's outburst, Oliver, the old orangutan from Ohio, ordered the obnoxious oaf and his offensive oboe out of the orchestra.

P reparing for a promenade near their palace in Paris, the patriotic poultry put on polka-dotted pants and peach pumps, then picked out pink parasols and purple purses.

They paraded proudly down the park path, pausing periodically to patronize the pert penguins peddling pizza or to prance to the peppy polkas played on piccolos.

Quentin Quail felt quite qualified to question the quartet of quahogs who'd been quibbling about their quarters on the quay. But he quit querying, quavered, and quickly became quiet when he was quashed by the queen.

R

osa Rabbit was roused from a rest by robbers removing the refrigerator in her Roman restaurant for resale in Rumania.

She raced from her room and roundly rebuked the rascals, but they rattled her resolve for revenge with their remorseful repentance.

Shortly after Sara Skunk set sail for Southampton on Sunday, a sudden savage squall sent her skiff smashing into the stern of a sloop skippered by Stanley Salamander.

The ships sank but Sara's supper surfaced, and she shared her salami salad sandwiches with Stanley. "Such a sandwich!" shouted Stanley. "So superbly satisfying! So smashingly scrumptious! So sublimely seasoned!"

Sara said that Stanley's speech was somewhat silly, and that the sandwiches were simply soggy from being submerged. They splashed shoreward, swapping stories of similar storms they'd seen at sea.

T

eresa Turkey tuned in turtle tennis on Tuesday, but that troublesome twosome, Terrence Terrapin from Texas and Taylor Tortoise from Tennessee, threw such terrible temper tantrums that Teresa terminated the tournament by tossing the television into the trash.

U

tterly uninspiring on the ukuleles, Ursula and her uncle were upstaged by the unicorns unicycling upside down under their umbrellas.

V

incent and Valerie Vulture, Vincent's valet, and the vacationing voles from Virginia were vaguely vexed when their voyage to Vesuvius to view the volcano and the various villas in the vicinity was vetoed by visitors from Venus who vanished with their vessel.

W

oodrow W. Wallop, who was wild about weight lifting, was out west in Washington when he went to Wilson's Gym to work out.

He told Wally Woodchuck and Willy Wombat that he wanted to wrestle, but they worried about the wisdom of wrestling with a wolf and wondered if Woodrow would be willing to wrestle Wendell, who was waiting to be weighed. Woodrow wagered his wristwatch and wallet he would win.

But when wedged under Wendell, a well-known wrestling whale from Walla Walla, he watched Willy and Wally withdraw with their winnings and wished he'd been wiser about that wager.

Xerxes Ox excused Rex from the exercise exhibition by the six expert executives after he became exhausted from excessive exertion.

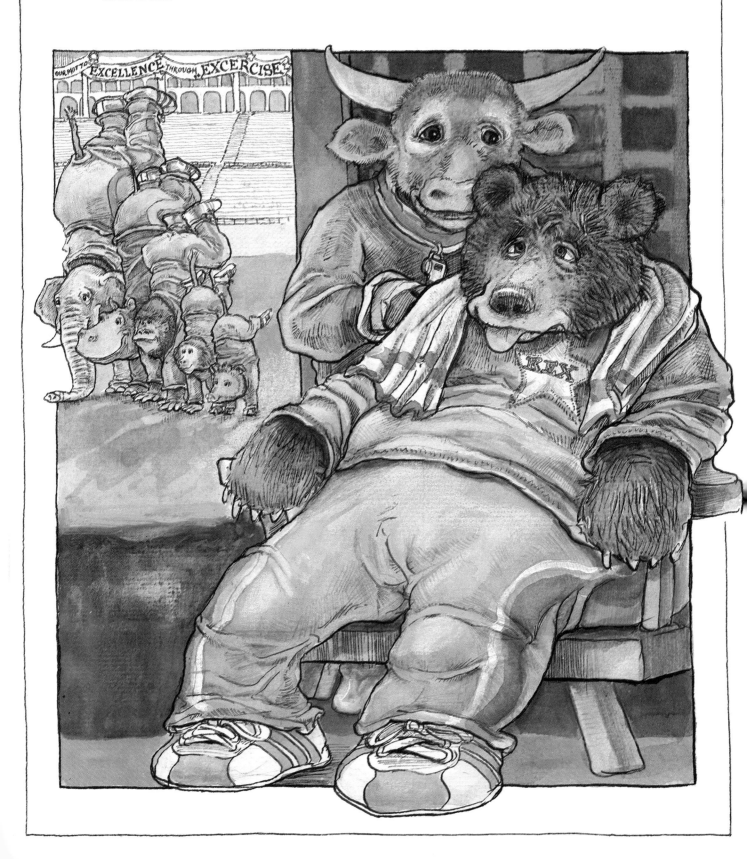

Yonder is Yugoslavia!" yelled the young yokel from his yawl, but the yak on the yellow yacht only yawned.

Z
-z-z-z-z-z-z-z-z-z-z-z-z-z-z-z-z-z-z-z-z-z-z-z-z-z-z-z-z-z-z-z-z-z-z-z-z-z-z-z-z-z-z-z-z-z-Z.